This igloo book belongs to:

....

igloobooks

Published in 2015
by Igloo Books Ltd
Cottage Farm
Sywell
NN6 0BJ
www.igloobooks.com

LEO002 0615
2 4 6 8 10 9 7 5 3 1
ISBN: 978-1-78440-736-0

Written by Melanie Joyce
Illustrated by Polona Lovsin

Printed and manufactured in China

I Love You, Too

igloobooks

You look so cute in the morning all snuggled up in bed,
as sunbeams shine on you, my little sleepyhead.

It makes me feel so happy when you say,
"Mummy, I love you."
Now, I'll tell you all the reasons why
I love you, too.

Sometimes you are very bouncy and love to jump around.

"Watch me, Mummy!" you cry, as you roll along the ground.

We play at hide-and-seek and
splash in puddles, too.

You love to squeal and run away
when I chase after you.

I love you because you want to play, no matter what the weather.

You giggle with your little friends, as you have fun together.

I love you because you say my stories
are the best you've ever heard.

You sit very still, without a sound,
listening to every word.

You give me lovely hugs,
which are squashy and
as warm as toast.

Your tickly kisses make
me giggle and I love
them the most.

I love you because you are very brave,
even when you cry.
I dab at your dribbly, trickly tears and
gently wipe them dry.

Sometimes we sit together,
in the evening light.
We watch the pale moon rise,
waiting for the night.

You are the most precious thing to me.
There is no one quite like you.
I know you will always love me and
I will always love you, too.

I love you,

Little Bunny